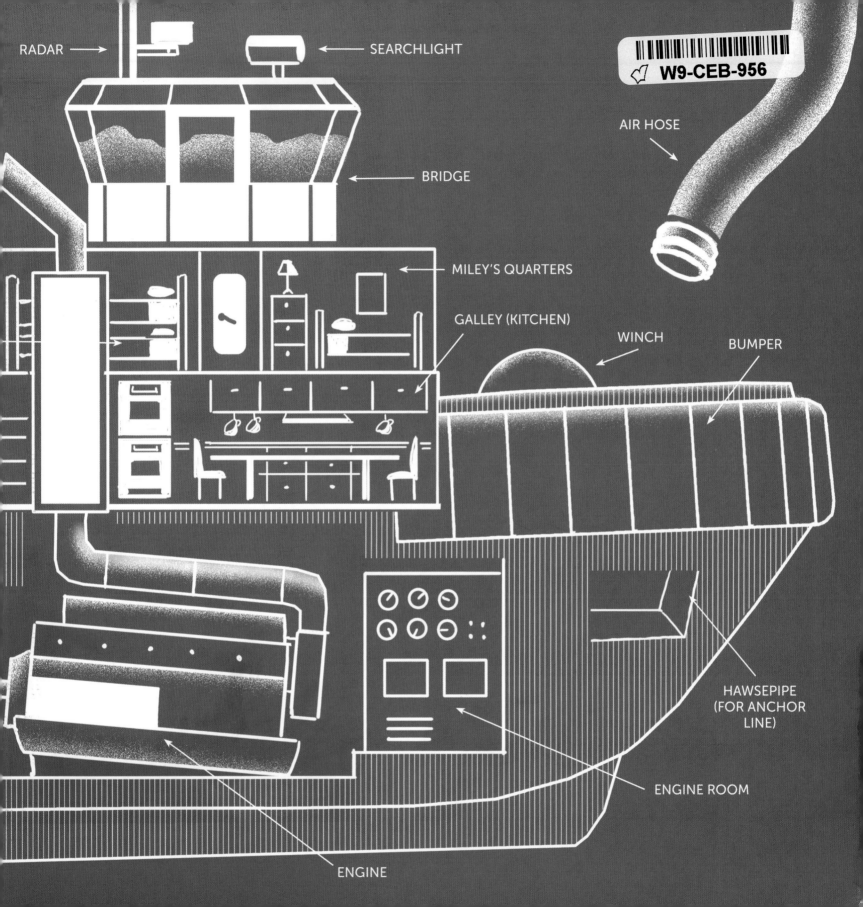

RADAR

SEARCHLIGHT

W9-CEB-956

AIR HOSE

BRIDGE

MILEY'S QUARTERS

GALLEY (KITCHEN)

WINCH

BUMPER

HAWSEPIPE (FOR ANCHOR LINE)

ENGINE ROOM

ENGINE

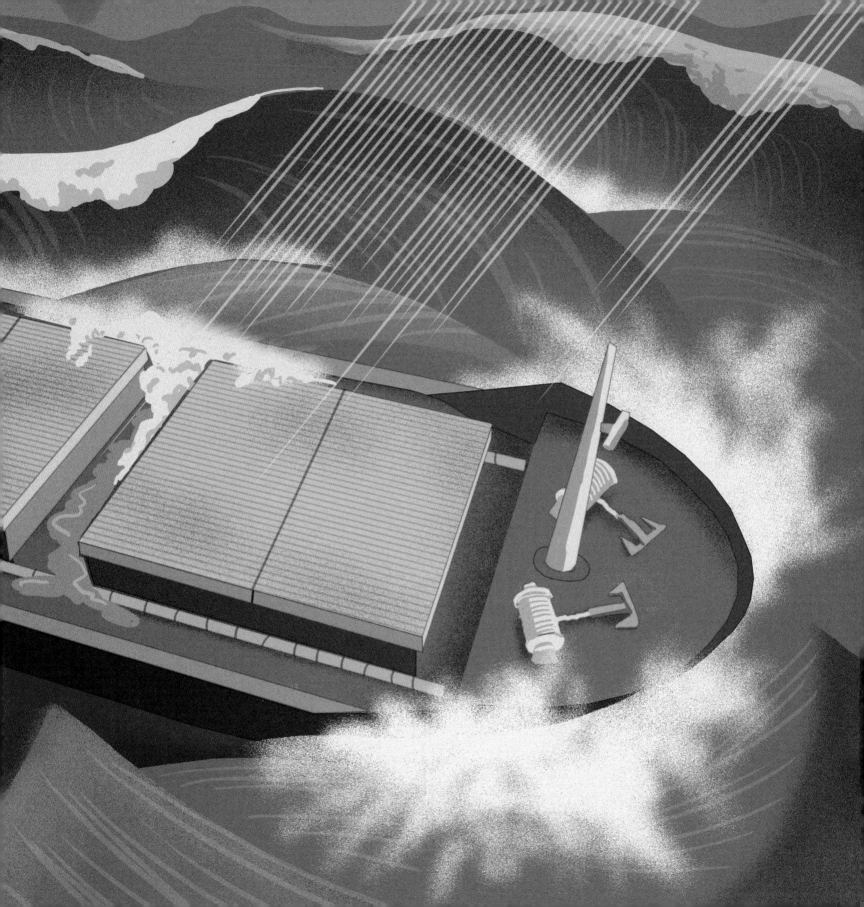

A ship is in trouble! The *Goliath* is fighting gale-force winds. It's hauling tons of iron, it's taking on water, and the engines have quit.

The crew calls for help!

BIG SHIP
RESCUE!

CHRIS GALL

NORTON YOUNG READERS

An Imprint of W. W. Norton & Company
Independent Publishers Since 1923

A rescue helicopter arrives to take the crew off the ship.

In these winds, it's tricky!

Now the *Goliath* is adrift without a crew.

Watch out!

Waves have driven the boat onto shore.

Salvage Master Miley is on the way! She captains the *Mighty Mackerel*.

Her team must make the ship safe and stop it from doing any more damage to the shore.

The *Mighty Mackerel* has two giant **engines**, two huge **propellers**, long **towlines**, and strong **winches**. This tugboat has power!

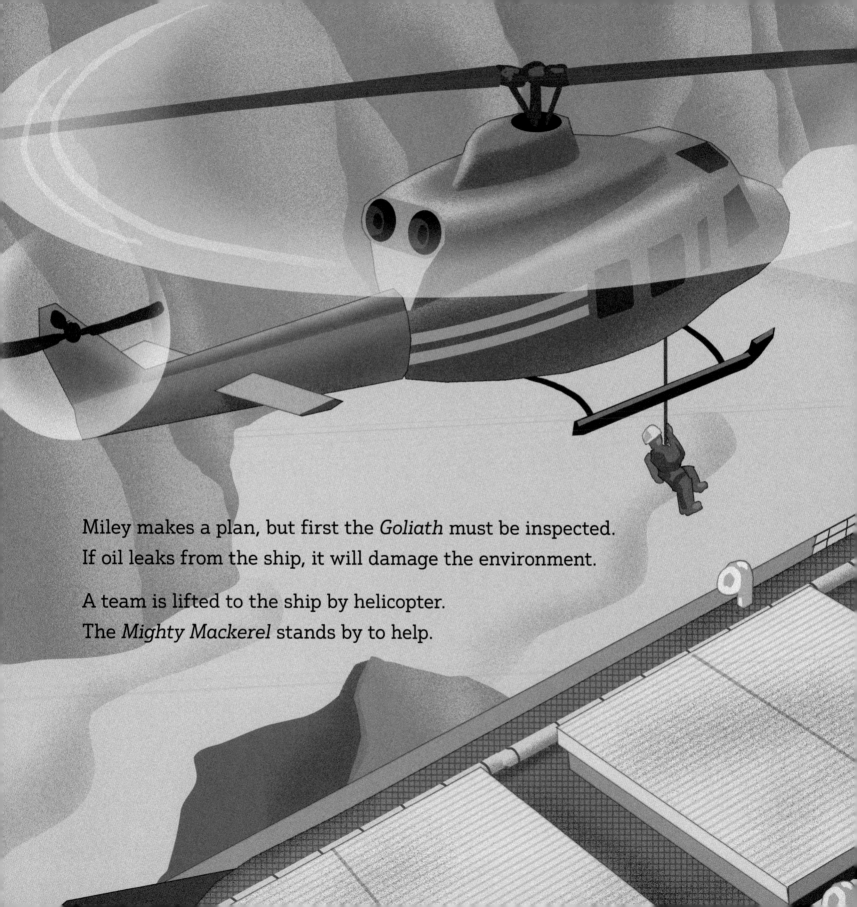

Miley makes a plan, but first the *Goliath* must be inspected.
If oil leaks from the ship, it will damage the environment.

A team is lifted to the ship by helicopter.
The *Mighty Mackerel* stands by to help.

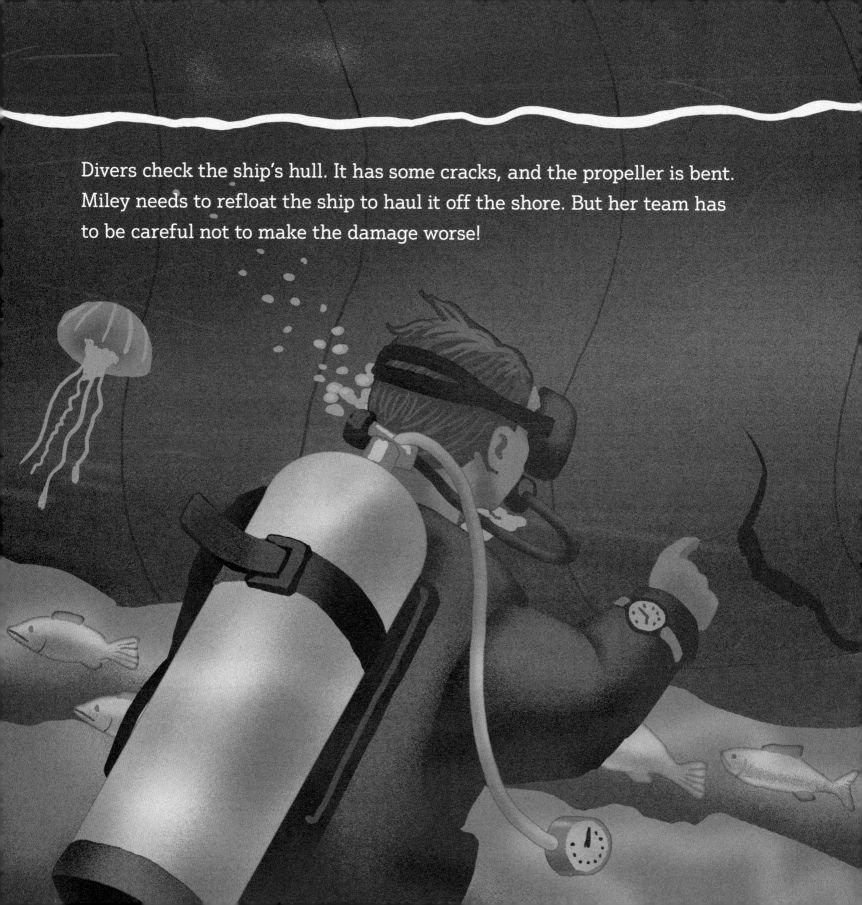

Divers check the ship's hull. It has some cracks, and the propeller is bent. Miley needs to refloat the ship to haul it off the shore. But her team has to be careful not to make the damage worse!

The salvage gear arrives. The team will need generators for power, compressors, air hoses, and welding tools.

The fuel oil is pumped into a barge. They don't spill a drop!

To lighten the ship, the cargo must be off-loaded.

Rocks and sand are dredged from under the ship.
The team is careful not to damage any coral.

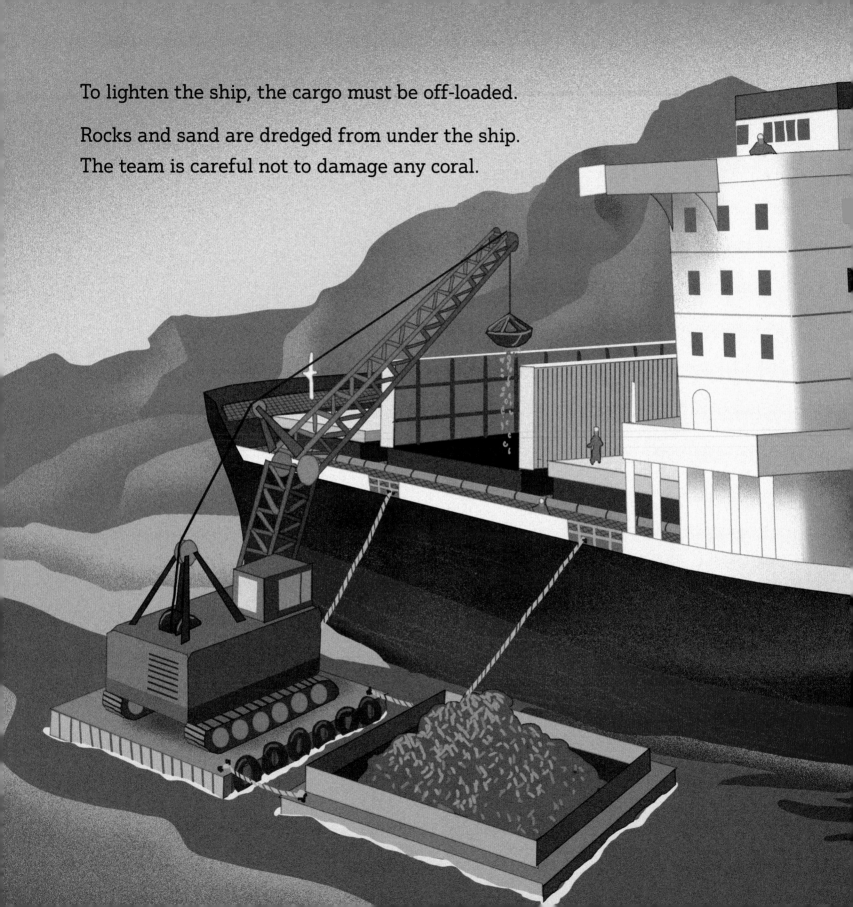

The cargo hatches are welded shut in a shower of sparks. Then the team pumps air into the holds. The air pushes out the water that has leaked inside, and helps the ship to float again.

It's time to set up for the tow. Towlines are thrown over the **bollards** on the *Goliath*, and the lines are lowered to the *Mighty Mackerel*.

Look out below!

Miley sets the **anchors** off the bow. Then she connects the winch to the towlines.

Two more tugs arrive to help. Everybody has to pull together.

The salvage team waits for high tide. The *Goliath* starts to shift!

Salvage Master Miley gives the command to hit the throttle and power up the winches. The aft winch pulls on the *Goliath*, the propellers push the boat forward, and the bow winch pulls on the anchors.

Pull! Pull! Pull!

Miley's got the power for the job!

Success! The giant *Goliath* slips off the shore and back to sea.

The *Mighty Mackerel* tows the *Goliath* to port. Harbor tugs help to dock the ship.

There's still hope for the *Goliath*. It can be repaired for more travels around the world.

It's been a long month of work for the salvage team. But the seas are calm and the weather fair. Salvage Master Miley is ready to head back to her home port.

It's so good to be home.

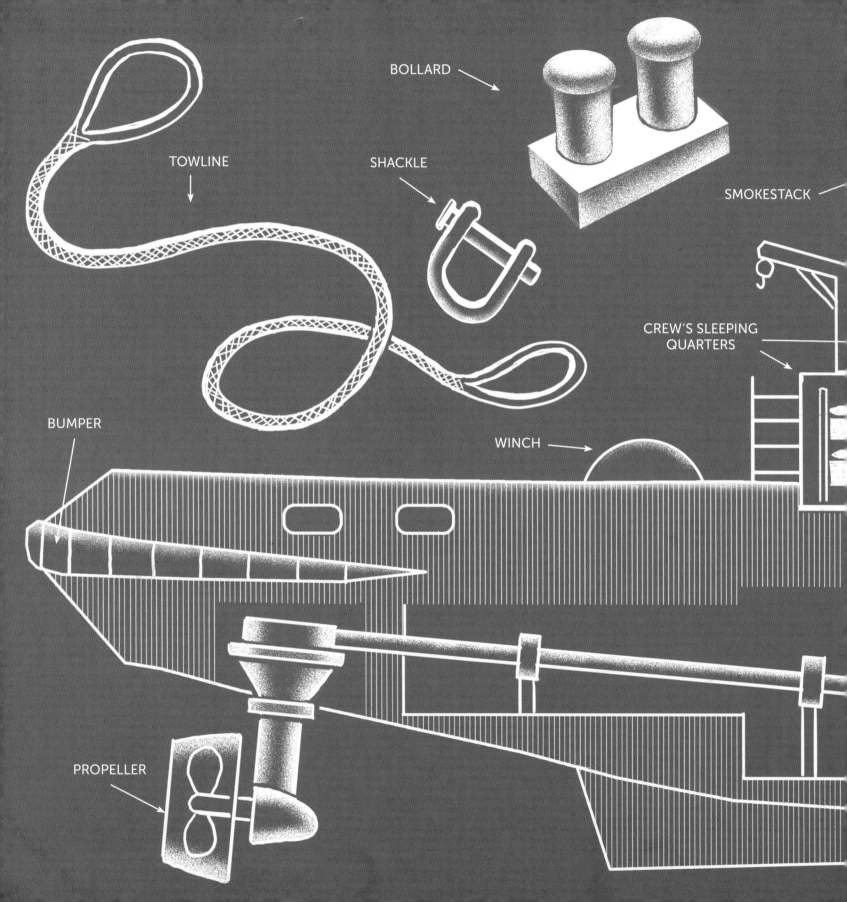

TOWLINE

BOLLARD

SHACKLE

SMOKESTACK

CREW'S SLEEPING
QUARTERS

WINCH

BUMPER

PROPELLER